A Legend of Elkapella

A Legend
of
Elkapella

JB Mounteer

ARPress
ILLUMINATING IDEAS
EMPOWERING VOICES

ARPress LLC
45 Dan Road Suite 5
Canton MA 02021
Hotline: 1(888) 821-0229
Fax: 1(508) 545-7580

Ordering Information:
Quantity sales. Special discounts are available on quantity purchases by corporations, associations, and others. For details, contact the publisher at the address above.

Printed in the United States of America.

ISBN-13:   Softcover   979-8-89330-581-4
                 Hardcover   979-8-89330-582-1
                 eBook   979-8-89330-583-8

Library of Congress Control Number: 2024901825

Thank you, Dad,
for never giving up on

Contents

PROLOGUE I

Chapter 1

THE TRIBE. 1

Chapter 2

THE LEGEND OF ELKAPELLA. 6

ELKAPELLA. 13

Chapter 3

SHEBA ELK. 15

Chapter 4

THE HUNT 18

Chapter 5

ANOTHER VIEW. 22

Chapter 6

A NEW ARRIVAL 28

Chapter 7

Final Understanding 39

Chapter 8

Dream?. 48

About the Author 51

PROLOGUE

ORDEN'S ARMS STRAINED as he lifted his body over the rocky ledge. "Thankful for those pushups now ma!" He shouted excitedly into the open sky over his shoulder. He had always been a fit young man of deep thoughts and rugged looks. When it came to working out his bod, he would rather climb a mountain than run on a treadmill. The thoughts of his moms teasing him, brought on a wide scruffy faced grin. "Thanks for the memory!" he shouted almost losing his grip. He flipped up his last leg and rolled onto his back, away from the cliffs edge.

When it came to working out his mind, he would rather read on a high peak overlooking a vast forest, or next to a bubbling brook, then in a stuffy study hall. His mind worked in many ways of logical thinking, so he not only dove into every book he came across, from ancient mythology, archeology, physicists to graphic novels and teenage fiction, which to Jorden, was very humorous. And he now found himself climbing a mountains top that has never been seen because of cloud cover. A mountain for him, that is shrouded in mystery. "Ugh, this week has been way more of a workout, then I thought."

Wiping the sweat from his forehead he grabbed his water bottle and GPS from his backpack, "Still nothing." he exhaled deeply. He looked back over the edge, down at what he had climbed. He was astonished how high he was. No one that he had heard of nor researched, had ever charted this mountains peak. He watched a large bird fly over the tree line far below him, "Sore high for me my friend!" he saluted. He placed his gadgets back in his pack and turned to face the cliff. He needed to find his next few foot holes, when he spotted a large crack in the cliff face. Carefully he slid himself along the narrow edge, until he reached it. He turned to face it and stepped inside.

Jorden could not believe his eyes. A giant smile grew on his scruffy face. The crack opened into a whole hidden world. He could see a great field surrounded by forest and a few plants he couldn't identify. An oasis surrounded and hidden from the world by a wall of rock. Like a world in the mouth of a large volcano. Jorden just stared, taking in everything he could see, astonished! He marveled at the forest that surrounded most of it, with all the different kinds of trees. Evergreens he expected to see in the region, but what looked like willows, exotic and eastern flora. He was looking at nothing he had ever seen, heard of, read about, or even dreamt of.

His eyes suddenly stuck on a single, very large mound in the center. The more he looked, the more out of place it looked. It did seem to be set in the middle of the field. He couldn't be sure with the tall grass and few trees between them. He waved a fly away and walked slowly towards it, scanning the ground the best he could.

The wind felt nice on his neck. He had spent the last few days hiking and he knew he didn't smell very good. He smiled when he felt the air temperature suddenly dropped. He took a deep breath of mountain air to confirm his suspicion. He had learned from years of motorcycle riding, that, that meant there was likely a river or body of water nearby. He could use a bath.

Just a few feet from the main mound, he found a small one. He went to sit down and quickly discovered it was not a mound, but an artifact. The dirt and moss pulled easily off reveling slick stone underneath. It looked as though nature had set a rug made of dirt and moss over her park bench. This strange rock stood as tall as his waist, it had a square bottom and smaller square top. The four slick sides were as smooth as glass and shined brightly in the sun. He quickly turned his attention to the large mound and excitedly started ripping off moss. Jorden guessed the large one had to be at least twelve feet tall, and at least as wide. The two megaliths looked like pyramids with their tops cut off.

After ripping off enough moss off the big section, he sat back on the small stone to scour it with his eyes, to search for markings. After a minute of staring, scratching his beard growth and other dirty sweaty places, he took out his binoculars and drifted slowly over the field. He watched the tree lines, the hills and plants growing on and around them. Trying to take in and force himself to remember every detail. He knew the chances of ever coming back to this magical place was not very good. A photograph has Nothing, on Life Experience.

He looked beyond the monolith, he could see some small hills, a shallow, probably great fly fishing, stream running through the field and disappearing into a forest. He couldn't see it, but he could hear, smell, and feel a large river, the stream would meet and become part of.

Jorden, reached down to tie his old worn hiking boots and something reflected, like a wink from the sun. He moved his boot to revel more of what looked like might be black onyx, a shiny black mineral. This beautiful piece had a very recognizable shape to Jorden. "It couldn't be!" he all but shouted. He looked around feeling a little insecure. He had not just shouted but jumped a little. His scruffy smile growing wider as he carefully wiped it clean. He had just found, a perfectly preserved arrowhead, Jorden, was ecstatic!

After the excitement and a hundred origin stories running through his mind, he set his attention to the largest gift of the day, as he stepped to the megalith and looked it over closer. Some of the rocks around looked like they had heated and colored from many fires and smoke.

He took his bandanna and slowly and gently brushed over the front where he first saw something. The moss came off easily, leaving only dark soil that brushed off almost as easy. The rock was smooth as glass. One large chunk fell off exposing a hand sized engraving, cracked in dry mud, all he could make out, was what looked like could be elk antlers and maybe some kind of flute. He placed his hand over it, needing to feel, as well as see this amazing ancient work.

"There are more treasures to find up here, " he thought. "Maybe even a story." He placed his hand on the glyph letting his finger feel the warm indention, trying to feel more of its contour. He suddenly realized he was still holding the arrowhead when it and the rock under his hand started to burn. They suddenly sent out a burst of warm white light, he could not let go. He squeezed his eyes tight to keep out the blinding light, and that's when he seen....

Chapter 1

THE TRIBE

N TOP OF A LARGE MOUNTAIN , its cliff topped peak, always hidden by clouds. In this hidden place, there lived ancient people. They had never seen another tribe of people. Other than those retired Koka who left, no one had seen the outside world. Only the Kokas, the retired wisemen, had ever wanted to leave their secluded home and the Kokas only left, to go teach.

Like many of the secluded groups, tribes, and villages around the world, they had their own language, traditions, and values. One of many unique to their own, especially one special legend.

Today the sky was filled with dark clouds moving with the wind down from the east cliff that continued around and surrounded their world. The air cooled as it passed over the river and into the village. The weather was not the best, but the air was filled with pride, excitement, music, and joy. The entire tribe sang, danced and played their flutes towards the heavens.

They danced around the council fire and ceremonial stone. Today was special. Today they would have a great ceremony, the hunters were to take their young boys on their first hunt.

The Koka, the wise man of the people, sat on a large megalithic rock in the center of the village. "The Center Stone," the Kokas called it, none knew when or how it was made. No one remembers its age. It has been used for all their ceremonies, as long as anyone could remember.

The Koka sat at the edge of his throne like seat, smiling down towards the blazing fire and the people, his family below. He sat slightly swaying to the music, watching them sing and dance. His own flute lay across his lap, waiting patiently for its turn to sing.

After a time, he raised his old, weathered fists high in the air and waved them back and forth. The smoke and the fire started to swirl and change shapes as it reached up towards him and the star lite sky. "My people," he said, in an old rough voice. "Today our sons will become men."

He started to swirl his outstretched fists, the smoke thickened and formed the shape of a large Elk tossing his antlers back and forth, sending smoke and ash out into the dark. The people of the village watched in awe, as the fire and shadow Elk rose in the air and drifted away in the breeze.

"Our sons shall go with their fathers." The old wise one continued. "They shall learn our hunter's ways and hunt our brother Elk, who dwell in the forest." He waved his fists through the fire and the smoke formed a giant grizzly bear running across the sky. "Remember young ones," he yelled, looking down at the boys that surrounded the special stone.

"To follow Elkapella's ways, he shall lead you to our Elk brothers." He smiled widely beneath his long-braided beard. He waved his arm around more, dancing with the fire, creating animals of all shapes and sizes.

He waved one hand at the fire and his fist with the other. He lifted his flute and did a little dance and special song. The fire sputtered higher and flickered, shooting bright sparks swirling deeper into the night sky. The smoke and sparks circled faster and faster around, twisting and dancing around themselves. With a sudden large crackle, a burst of flames shot up in a swirling tunnel.

When the light faded down there was one large form. It was darker than the night, circled by flame and sparks dancing in thick grey smoke. It was the shimmering dark form of Elkapella.

The smoke and ash figure loomed over them, looking down at the tribe. His head and body, neither man nor Elk, but a combination of both. His great antlers hung down his back as he raised his tribal flute. He played an almost silent melody for the ear, both the body and the trees roaring behind them, could hear every note. The young boys watched in awe as Elkapella, rose higher in the air he seemed to motion for them to follow as he drifted away.

The wise man stood on his rock and pointed in the direction that Elkapella disappeared. "Elkapella has shown us which direction to find our Elk brothers." he said softly. "Our brothers who will share their meat and coats with us." One of the hunter's snorted his disbelief and folded his ceremonially painted arm's. The Koka looked at him, sadness, and disappointment in his eyes. The hunter's name was Elk-grandson, and he was the Koka's son. "You still disbelieve in Elkapella's way's my son." The Koka gestured towards the still fading ashes falling in the sky.

Elk-grandson shrugged, tightened his quiver and casually blew offff a spark that landed on his shoulder. "There are many truths to things you say my Koka." He angerly snapped another spark from the air. "The rest, is an old tale father, to trick our people into believing that animals are our equal brothers." He pulled on his leather vest and pounded his fist on his chest. "They are not our brothers; they are just stupid beasts, to eat and cloth our people!" he flipped his long black braids over his shoulder in deviancy. "They are nothing more!" The wise older man, slide off the holy stone and approached his son.

"Don't you remember the legend of Elkapella, my angry one?" he asked placing his hand on Elk-grandson's shoulder. The hunter pushed his father's hand away. "That's all it is father," he scowled. "Just a legend!" He walked over to where the young boys sat near the holy rock and placed a hand on his son's shoulder. "And I don't want you filling Eagle- heart's head with your silly old ways."

Eagle-heart, named after his mother Eagle-eyes. Her name came from her gift's. She could see things that no one else could and at times see what is to come tomorrow. They said she must have an eagle's eye. A third eye. He did not remember much of her; she had died when he was very young. He knew where his name came from, but he had always wondered where his father had gotten his.

Receiving a name was very important to their people. A Koka could tell someone's name within days of birth, and everyone had a story for their name. People would celebrate telling their names song, through song and dance. It bothered Eagle-heart that he could not hear his father's name song. Knowing someone's name, is only learning to make a sound. Knowing a person's song, is truly knowing them. Maybe his father didn't yet feel he was old enough to learn it by heart.

"But father," Eagle-heart, said looking up with hopeful eyes. "We should listen to Grandfather, he is the Koka!" he looked to his grandfather. "Grandfather," he said excitedly, as he loved any story. "Tell us the legend again!" He reached up and took hold of his father's hand. "Maybe it will help you remember father!" Elk-grandson squeezed his son's hand back. He cared very much for his boy; he just didn't want him raised in his father's old ways. He looked down at his son "It's just a story," he said softly. "a story of old ways, told by an old man." he wanted to scowl at him but could only manage a sad stare. "An old man that has told the story so many times, that he believes it to be true and is desperately trying to keep them alive!"

The Koka shook his head sadly at his son, the worry for his son's future showing in his weathered eyes. "Some stories are true my angry one, so open your heart and mind my son."

He turned back and started playing his flute. He continued playing as he stepped back onto the ceremonial rock. "Listen my people. It is time." his arms raising in the air again, one fist clenched.

"What I am about to tell you began on the same special day!" His eyes looked up to the dark sky, these ceremonies are not just for our son's journeys into manhood. His hands went from playing his flute to his hands dancing, all moving the smoke, fire, and spark lights. Everyone's eyes were drawn in as the flute and lights danced into new shapes and sounds. Like through Jorden's arrowhead, they could see back through time. "This is not just our story," his fists clenched tighter, and the fire and smoke thickened. "This is our legend."

Chapter 2

THE LEGEND OF ELKAPELLA

ON THE SAME ANCIENT STONE, in another earlier time, their stood older wise man. Below him the tribe's hunter's and sons elaborate notes echoed from their flutes. They danced and drummed as they left the celebration. Tossing their torches into council fire and checking their weapons of flint and bone strapped on, ready for quick release. Their quivers filled with arrows hanging on their backs. They danced and sang until they reached the outer edge of their village, when they came to a large ditch and mound that follows the tree line around, everyone stopped. No sound, no movement. After all they were no longer celebrating. They were hunting. Pellii, one of the young boys was very nervous and scared. Pellii had heard many tales from the hunter's, some stories of blood and hunters lives lost. Some were of hunter's being attacked by these deadly beasts. Stabbed by antlers, mauled by large bears, and even being shot by a friend's accidental arrow or spear. Everything down to a slip of a knife and cutting open their own leg, while just cleaning out the animal.

He had always been taught and understood that animals were just beasts for food. Here just so man could have meat, leather, sinew, and the tools they need. But before when the hunters would bring home animals after a hunt. Pelli would look into their big brown eyes and see sadness or fright frozen in them. Sometimes even what looked like tears. He could not help but wonder if there was a chance, that they could feel, what he could.

Pellii straightened his back and lifted his chin. No matter if he felt bad for them, they were on a hunt. His father was by his side, and he had a job to do. He must bring home meat, for without it, his family would not survive the winter to come. Pelli, was careful with every step he took. Scanning the ground for signs like his father had taught him. He looked over to his father that was doing the same.

Pella smiled back to his son. He was proud of him. It looked like he was using some of the many small things, that after time, turn into great knowledge. He had imparted to Pelli, that the smallest of things, have the largest effect on everything. When hunting, any indent in the earth could be a hoof print, a sign of its condition, every broken branch and leaf, a passing point. That a small variation in smell, could be change in wind direction. He taught him these things and much more.

Pella stopped abruptly, throwing out his arm to stop his son from falling forward and gestured to his ear. "Close your eyes and open your other." He tapped his forehead. "Reach out with it and your ears. Everything has a vibration and like the flute and taunt string of a bow, vibration is sound." he leaned closer to his young boy. "Your own vibration is connected to them all. Every sound that rides on the wind."

Pellii closed his eyes. He tried to stretch his ears out to the air. "I hear a long note father," he whispered. "It sounds like someone is playing part of the "Elkapella song!" he said a little louder than he wanted too. He looked down at his own flute. "It, Its.."

Pella nodded down at him. "It was an Elk."

Pellii could not hide his excitement. He had one hand over his mouth and the other on his flute. Waiting, trying not to let out a sound.

His eyes begging his father to give him the ok, to talk back to the beast. His hand held ready on his flute.

Pella with one hand knocked an arrow in his bow, "It is a cow calling to her calf." he said quietly moving forward. With his other hand, he gave a short blow on his flute. The note matched the Elks perfectly.

Pellii placed his fingers on his flute where he saw his father's. "Can I try?" he whispered kneeling next to him.

Pella listened to the breeze for a moment and sniffed the air. "Go ahead my son." he whispered. "Hold your tongue up, then a quick blow."

Pellii took in a short breath and blew. But the sound that came out was nothing like his father's, it was a high pitched and long sound. He winced at the sound he had made. "Sorry father," he said looking at his flute. "I.. i." Pella laughed softly and patted his little man's shoulder. "It's ok," he winked. "what you just did, took me two years to master." he winked. "You just bulged my boy."

There was a loud crashing in the trees in front of them. Sounded like something huge was tearing down every tree in its path. Pella smiled down at his son. "You just challenged a bull Elk to a fight." patting his boys head a little harder than he meant too. Both were very excited. "Now get behind that tree!" he waved. "He's mad and when he gets here, I don't want you in the open or anywhere in his sights." He looked in his sons' eyes. "These beasts will run you down, so stay down."

Pellii, quickly did as his father said, he did not want to be gouged by Elk antlers or trampled by their sharp split hooves. The crashing grew louder and louder and with every snap of a tree branch, Pelli jumped. He had never been so scared in his life. Sweat dripped into his eyes and his heart was beating out of his chest. He tried to reach an arrow, but his small hands were shaking to bad.

He watched as his father crept to the middle of the small clearing and knelt facing the thunderous crashing. Pella pulled back his bow string and took aim. With a loud explosion of branches and leaves, an enormous Elk burst out of the trees line.

Pellii could see the steam shoot out its large nose with each pounding breath. Its large antlers didn't slow it down. Its thick beams curves and points skimmed through the trees as if they were not even there.

The dust and strong scent of the beast that his father had told him about, it burned like fire in his nose, making him sneeze. The Elk gained speed as it ran straight for Pella, it's heavily muscled legs and hooves dug into the earth, ripping, and throwing chunks of dirt, grass, and rock out of the earth.

Pellii was frightened for his father. With a sudden burst of courage, he reached back, took out an arrow and knocked it, in one swift motion. He had practiced and pulled on it every day for months to build up his strength, now he was glad he did. He let the arrow fly.

The arrow flew like a star bursting through the heavens, hitting the Elk with a loud thump. The arrowhead sank deep into its front leg. The massive Elk didn't even slow down. Pellii looked at his father, who was as still as a boulder. Fear for his father erupted from every pore as the Elk was almost on top of him.

Pella never moved or took his eyes off the bull elk burrowing towards him. With a loud cry he let his arrow fly! With the same loud thump, it struck the beast right in the middle of its massive neck. The Elk still didn't slow down, and he had seen Pellii's arrow hitting it in its leg did not either. Instead, these just seemed to make him mad and speed him up. Pella was reaching for another arrow when the large Bull Elk ran right over him.

"Father!" Pellii screamed, watching as the Elk kept running and disappearing into the trees. He raced to his father; his fear soared through his body like icy pin pricks. When he got to his father, he knelt down beside him. Pella was moaning loudly and holding his chest. "Father are you alright?" he cried.

Pella sat up with surprising speed. "Come!" he ordered and ran stumbling after the bleeding beast.

Pellii stood on shaking legs and waited for his head to clear as his father and the Elk disappeared into the darkness of the forest. Once he got going, it was easy for him to follow, when he could hear them crashing through the foliage, but soon they were too far ahead of him to hear. He stopped and tried to stretch out his hearing, but it was no use, the sound was gone. But strong smell was still in the air, but he couldn't tell which way it was coming from. He sighed and bent down to look for signs. There was a small patch of bright red blood and a hole where the beast's hoof had torn through the dark earth. He started to move forward keeping his senses alert and one eye on the ground. He found blood high on tree trunks where the Elk had brushed through. He was amazed how big it was. The blood patches were starting to get thicker and the smell stronger. He knew he was getting closer.

Suddenly his ears picked up a small sound just ahead of him. It wasn't a loud thrashing, it sounded like brushing of leaves. He slowly crept forward an arrow knocked in his bow. He could hear deep, heavy breathing, coming from massive lungs. He peeked through the trees and gasped.

Lying against a tree trunk was the huge Elk. It still had the two arrows sticking out of its chest, in its front leg and one in its neck. The sight of the bloody Elk is not what made him gasp. Lying alongside the Elk was his father Pella.

Pella's arm was around the Elk's great neck where his flint knife was protruding. His other arm was trying to stop the blood from flowing out of the Elk's chest. His own chest was bleeding where the Elk had trampled him and one of the Elk's large antlers was lodged into his stomach. Their blood flowed to the forest floor and combined into one large puddle. Pella reach over and squeezed the Elk's neck in a loving embrace, and he started to cry.

"Father!" Pellii cried running over to them. "What happened?" he reached down and touched his father's strong shoulder. "What can I...

How can I..." he stuttered not knowing how to help his father. "Should I go find help?"

Pella looked up at his son with tear filled eyes and grasped his hand. "No, my son," he said in a windy whisper. "It's too late my brave one." He looked back to the Elk and whispered something into its large ear.

To Pellii's surprise, the Elk looked straight at him. The Elk's large brown eye was filled with sadness and to his surprise, tears.

Pella looked back to his son. "I have been so, so wrong my son," he said sadly, "Me and my brother have been talking and I have been wrong in what I have taught you." He slid his bloody hand down the Elks long jaw.

Pellii was confused. "But you don't have a brother father." he said wiping a tear from his eye.

Pella laughed causing himself to cough. "But I do." he whispered patting the Elk's neck. "The animals of the forest are not soulless beasts as I so crazily thought." He rested his head on the Elk's massive shoulder. "They are our brothers."

He then pointed to a young bull Elk they had not seen. It had been watching, hiding in the trees. "You also have a brother."

Pellii looked at the small Elk, then knelt down next to his father. "But I don't understand father." he sniffled.

Pella took his son's hand and placed it over the Elks heart. "Feel that my son," he said, "his heart beats just like ours. Look into his eyes and you will see he has a spirit just like ours." Pella smiled at his son. "I have taken my brother's life, and he has also taken mine."

"No father!" Pellii cried throwing his arms around his father.

Pella embraced his son. "From now on you must listen to your grandfather, always respect these brothers of ours." he said softly. He took a slow deep breath. "All of the animals that live among us, all of the creatures that live in this forest are our family." he patted the great

Elk's neck again. "You must always thank them when they give us their meat for food, thank them for their skins for our clothes and shelter." He looked his son straight in the eye. "You must never, never disrespect them my son." A tear fell from his father's eye. "I was wrong."

Pellii watched in disbelief as his fathers and Elk's blood flowed down from their chests and onto the forest floor. Their blood combined, swirled into one pool. He watched as together: they both took their last breath. He laid his hand on his father's bloody chest and started to cry. The young Elk in the trees let out a loud cry and lowered his head

ELKAPELLA

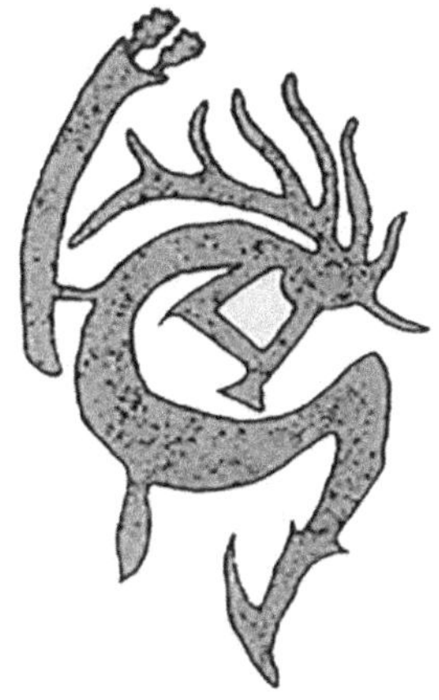

ELLII, LAID THERE FOR WHAT seemed like hours, hoping pleading, and praying this was a nightmare. He felt a small breeze start to blow. He lifted his head to see the leaves around them start to swirl in the air, then around his father and the elk. He could feel them getting warmer until it grew unbearable. He jumped up and backed away, not even noticing that he was next to the young Elk. The elk didn't seem to notice either. The breeze grew to wind, growing stronger and stronger, twisting, and twirling the fallen leaves and debris around them. A light started to grow around them until it was too bright for Pelli, to look at. He covered his eye's and ear's, the wind growing to a roar.

The light and sound grew and twisted until it exploded in a loud burst. The light dimmed and the wind died down to a soft breeze. Pellii slowly opened his eyes. Again, gasped at what he saw.

Floating in the breeze, feet off the ground, it was his father and the elk. They were glowing with energy, circling around them. He watched in awe as his father and the Elk slowly spun into one ball of light. The wind suddenly stopped, and the light dimmed. A large black figure floated in front of Pellii, it was a dark form. A black silhouette that looked half man, half Elk.

Pellii started to back away more, almost tripping over the small elk that stood beside him. The being reached out its hoof like hand. "Don't be frightened my son." he said in a deep, ghostly voice. "I am still your father my brave one, and I am also my brother."

Pellii rubbed his dust and tear-filled eye's. "What are you?" he asked, stepping closer. He felt no fear from it.

The black figure let out a deep but soft laugh, that encoded through the forest. "I am Elkapella my son," he said rising higher in the trees. "I am here to show our people and our brothers of the forest many things, things that they are ready for." He pointed down at him with what looked like a shadow of his father's flute. "You must teach our people, tell them what I have said. If they follow my ways and respect our brothers, I will always lead them to what they need." Elkapella reached out his strange hand again. "Take hold young man." he said softly. Pellii reached up and grasped the shadowy hand, half expecting it go through his like smoke. His hand started to tingle and grow hot. When Elkapella let go, he looked at his palm. His fingers were red from the heat and in the center of his palm, was the embedded black silhouette, of Elkapella.

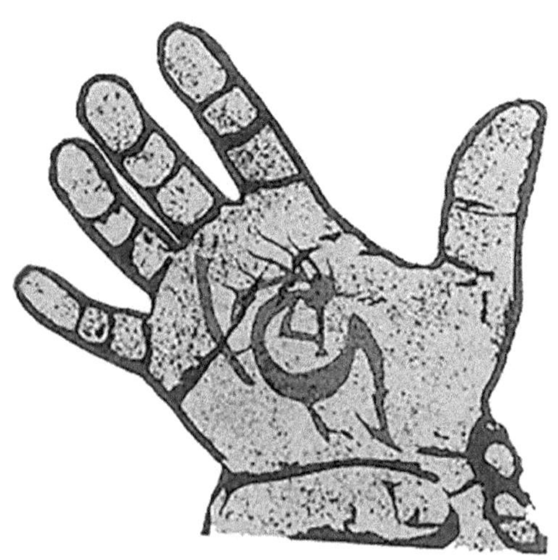

Chapter 3

SHEBA ELK

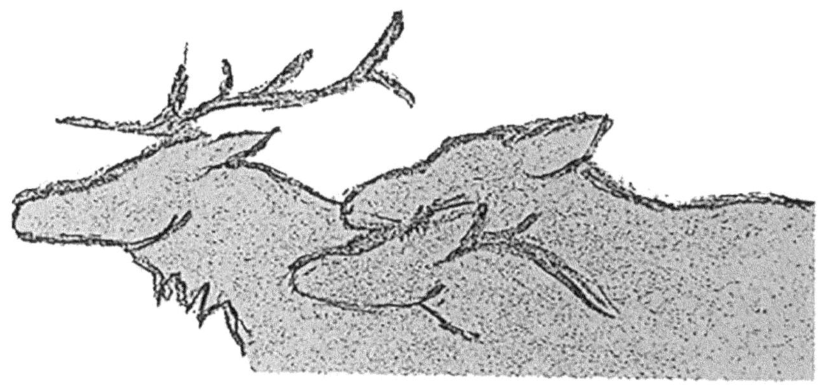

SHEBA WOKE AND STRECHED out her long elk legs and shook the dirt from her thick coat. She opened her big brown eyes and blinked them to adjust to the early morning light. She was laying in the edge of the thick forest that had been her home since she was a small calf. She took in a deep breath of the crisp clean mountain air. She could immediately smell the plentiful grasses, flowers, and trees around her, but also the rich earth and dew beneath her hooves. She could even smell her mother and father close by.

She stood and looked out at the large meadow in front of her. The dew glistened with the sunlight as it slowly filled the field. As beautiful as it was, Sheba felt a sudden sadness grow in her. The sweet, crisp grass there was almost gone, and there was the familiar chill coming down the cliffs and over the rivers. She knows her father will want to move on soon. The cold and hardships of winter was coming, and they needed to eat and store as much fat as possible through the summer, to keep them warm from the long, cold winter, and their food was almost gone.

Sheba shook the negative thoughts from her mind did a little hop to shake the dew from her feet and tail, then happily start eating the wet grass. She loved the taste of this meadow's grasses, especially when it started to seed. Almost as good as the purple flowers.

She looked over to see her father and mother grazing next to the trees. Her father was one of the largest of the bull elk. Her eyes focused on his thick antlers, that spread wide as he raised his head to look around. His large neck turned back and forth, his long ears meandering across batting flies away and listening to the surroundings. He yawned, showing his two large ivory teeth.

"Hey, father!" she called out as she noticed them. "If deer are just our smaller brother line, why do they not have that type of teeth?"

He leaned his massive head and neck back, filled his great lungs with air and let out a beautiful bellow that slid from a deep low to high pitch and back again. Like a giant horn it bounced off the mountains and sliced through the trees. He looked back at her lifting one eyelid.

"Got it!" she laughed.

Sheba walked to the river that was close by. The water felt great, she slapped her head around splashing herself. The water tasted clear as the blue morning sky. She glanced down the river and saw two large Bears playing and catching their fill of fish, they needed to store up much fatter, for they take long winter slumbers. Sheba had made friends like them and would miss them all for a time. Others she would never see, they had been taken by the two-legged ones.

Her father had tried to explain to her some of the Elkapella's teachings.

Especially those teachings of the two-legged creatures. She loved the lore and mysteries of Elkapella, but Sheba, did not want to listen about them. As far as she cared, they were just cruel, soulless beasts.

Sheba walked over and nudged her mother's neck. "Good morning mother." she said, blinking her long eyelashes on her large brown eyes.

Her mother smiled lovingly and nodded towards her father. "He seen Elkapella, today," she said looking back to Sheba. "So will be leaving soon."

Sheba ignored the leaving part, concerned more with the legendary Elkapella.

She looked around excitedly, her eyes wide and tail wagging furiously, she had always wanted to see Elkapella with her own eyes. She was sure, she would see him one day and maybe that was today.

She had heard the legend of Elkapella, almost every day since she was born.

She didn't know where he came from or where he went, but he had always been there.

Sheba's father knew more than he would tell her about the legend. The ways he always told it; it was like he was there to see it himself. She could tell by the look in his eye's that he always wanted to say more, but something would continually stop him, before he could speak the words.

He told her that one day long ago; the hunters were mean, cruel, and ruthless beasts. They would seem to slaughter animals, even when they had enough and were fat and full. They would always take more than they needed. He told her that when Elkapella came, that all changed. Elkapella had also taught the hunters how to listen to the forest and all of us that live in this world with them. They were not the only creatures here, that matter.

"Shandee, Sheba," her father shouted, his dark eyes scanning into the trees.

"We must go!"

Sheba's mother looked worried too as she used her nose as well as eyes to see beyond the trees and stepped closer to Sheba's father. "You smell something too don't you." she whispered.

Sheba's father nodded. "Elkapella had shown us to move already," he started to walk into the dark of the woods. "I thought we had more time to gather."

Chapter 4

THE HUNT

HE KOKA FINISHED TELLING "The legend of Elkapella", spread out his arms and pointed in the direction that the smoke Elkapella drifted. "To the hunt my young ones!" he shouted into the wind.

The people of the celebration kept singing as they raised their flutes in celebration. They danced around the council fire until the hunters reached the circles around the encampment. Just as the hunters headed into the forest.

Eagle-Heart was nervous and excited at the same time. He knew that the Elkapella they had seen, was just the Koka's creation of smoke and fire, it still encouraged him in his heart. He had been looking forward to this day for as long as he could remember. He tightened his quiver strap, checked his bow string, and his knife that were hanging on his belt. He had to run to keep up with his father. That's when he realized that he didn't have his flute!

All his people carried a flute, starting from birth. They played them to celebrate, and they played them to mourn. They were colorful people that had songs and notes for every aspect of their lives. The unique flutes were a symbol of their people and the central tool for the world around them. His grandfather had even been using it in his Koka trainings. Teaching them strange sounds, notes that would help their crops grow and songs, that would help their people even have children. His favorite was the unique sounds, notes that could tell the rivers which way to go and the rocks where to rest. If he lost it, it is as losing a part of himself. How could he even hunt without it??

Ahead, his father was walking fast through the trees, dodging low branches, watching the ground for signs. "Hurry my son," he whispered louder than he wanted too. "Keep your ears open, you will be able to hear the Elk calls, they are the same as the flute. Keep your eyes open, nose open to the air." He pointed ahead. "When we are close you will be able to smell their strong scent." he laughed "trust me."

Eagle-heart tried to keep his senses alert as best he could, he did not want to disappoint his father. As he looked around, he noticed that they were heading away from where Elkapella had motioned for them to follow. "Father," he whispered. "Elkapella went in the other direction."

Elk-grandson stopped and looked back at his son. "I saw nothing, you're listening to your grandfather's foolish ways." he said, more angrily than he meant too. "It's getting in your head. It is an exaggerated story Eagle-heart, not a legend!" He knelt down and placed his strong hand on Eagle-heart's shoulder. "You must trust in your senses my son," he said quietly "not to my father's senseless talk." He patted Eagle-hearts, head. "Come on my son, we must go before it gets to hot, the Elk will not move once it has entered into the thick trees to keep cool."

Eagle-heart nodded and started to follow his father, when he saw a black figure out of the corner of his eye. "Father!" he almost shouted. "Look, it's Elkapella!" He pointed excitedly, as it disappeared into the trees to the side of them.

Elk-grandson looked back to where his son was pointing and shook his head. "Elkapella is a story." He groaned trying to keep his temper in check. He didn't like to talk in anger. "I don't see Elkapella," he looked over the path more. "But... that does look like a way to the other east meadow and sounds like the river heads that way too," he smiled. "Good job my boy."

Eagle-heart was astounded, he had finally seen Elkapella. As they turned, he wondered why his father hadn't seen him. Then he remembered his Koka telling him, "Only ones who respect his ways, will be able to see Elkapella" Today his father did not.

His father motioned for him to slow down, so he watched his moccasins, carefully placing each step.

Elk-grandson reached back, slowly pulled an arrow from his quiver and knocked it in his bow. He tapped Eagle-heart's shoulder and pointed at his nose. He knew what his father meant; he could smell the very strong scent of Elk nearby. He put an arrow in his bow as well and adjusted the feathers. He wanted to make sure it would fly straight, because he knew his hands were not going to stop shaking.

They stopped, spotting a smaller clearing just ahead of them through the trees. There was a sudden loud crack of a thick branch breaking. They seen the bull elk walking towards them. Eagle-heart watched as the Elk would take a few steps then stop and sniff the air. His large head and his antlers, turned back and forth as he listened for any unusual sound and watched for any movement.

Just behind the bull, there stood a large cow and a smaller one. Elk-grandson pulled back his bow string and took aim at the bull Elk.

Eagle-heart could feel his heart start to race, as he too pulled back his bow string. With a sudden swish, he let go of his string.

Before he knew it his father was up like a flash, running to the elk. Eagle-heart thought he would beat the arrow. He ran, trying with everything he had to keep up, but the trees were too thick, and the earth covered with many tracks, leaves and paths. Before he knew it, he was lost.

Eagle-heart's heart was starting to pound more with fear, then excitement.

He stopped to take a breath and gather his thoughts. Thick trees surrounded him like a tight blanket that he could barely see through. The light from the sun was having a hard time trying to break through the thick branches. He could see only a few feet in, on either side of himself. The trees and half fallen logs confused his sense of direction. He couldn't even tell if he was walking up the hills or down. The fear grew deep inside him like a rush of cold arrowheads piercing his insides. His stomach tightened in knots.

He took in a calming breath and opened his eyes to see fresh Elk tracks that had ripped through the ground in front on him. Eagle-heart felt a little better now, he knew if he followed them, he would find his father.

Chapter 5

ANOTHER VIEW

SHEBA, STARTED TO FOLLOW her parents into the trees, when she suddenly smelled something strong. Her father and mother smelled it too, it was the scent of hunter's. Her father's head was swaying back and forth, trying to find out which direction the scent was coming from. He looked back. "Run!" Without hesitation Sheba ran as fast as her large strong legs could go, she knew what to do. Her father had taught her well, he had told her to run as fast as she could and as far as she could, to circle and backtrack, confuse the hunters, and meet back in a hidden spot further down the river.

Suddenly she heard a sound that sent cold shivers down her spine. She had heard that sound before, it was the sound of an arrow shooting from a bow. She will never forget that vibration. The beasts had shot at her parents. The fear raced through her body like a river rushing down the mountain. She was running so fast, over her heavy breathing, wind, and braking foliage, she couldn't hear if the arrow had hit anything.

She reached out in her thoughts. She called to Elkapella, that he would keep her parents safe. She did what she was taught several times before she was too tired to run anymore. She collapsed on the ground next to a large tree panting heavily. Blinking the tears from her eyes.

She caught a whiff of its scent again. But this time it was different, it wasn't as strong, yet she could hear the hunter was closer. She looked up just in time to see a hunter step out of the trees and freeze in front of her.

This beast was different from the ones she had only caught glances of before. This one was smaller, a lot smaller it had the look of fear in his eyes. He was looking right at Sheba, as if it feared her. The beast was scared of her.

Memories of lessons ignored came flooding back to her. Elkapella's teachings of man. She sensed a change in the air, and she seen the look in his eyes had also changed. Neither of them was scared, neither wanted to run. She could see he might be remembering the teachings as well.

Sheba couldn't quite tell what, but something of the man resembled Elkapella's form. Sheba and the small hunter stared at each other for a long time studying, learning all they could learn with their eyes and nose. Sheba was surprised that she didn't feel afraid of this hunter anymore. Instead, she felt safe, a strange calm that she would always be protected by him. This was very strange.

The man smiled at Sheba and quickly placed his arrow and knife away.

He chatted something softly to her, but it was sound combinations that she couldn't understand.

Sheba scratched the ground and nodded her head trying to let him know, that she knew, he was trying. The man eyes narrowed with lines appearing on the sides, showing he smiled at her. But strangely his mouth went wide showing some of his teeth.

Suddenly he waved his hands and stomped his foot. He chattered more strange sounds at her, slapped the side of his head, and laughed.

She knew that he had just thought of something, and by the way he was acting, it was something he should have thought of right away. She laughed a little in her head.

He pulled out a colorful, carved dead tree branch. It looked like it had been hollowed out and holes carefully bored along the sides and top. It something beautiful, like Sheba had never seen before. She had never seen anything that was made by the beasts. By man. But it stunk.

The branch itself did not smell to bad. It smelled mostly of wood, bone, and even shiny metals of the earth. The strap, smelled much like the rest of his distasteful dead skin covers. They wear over their own skin.... Beasts indeed.

The young man raised the dead branch to his mouth and started to exhale into it. The sound that came out surprised Sheba. Some of the sounds matched a mother crying for her lost child. Another sounded like a child searching for their parents. Sheba raised and shook her head and stared harder into the hunter's trying eyes. She wanted to know more of this different man's spirit.

She wondered why he would tell her of a mother and child in pain?

The small hunter smiled, then made the sound of the sad child again and pointed to her. Sheba knew that the hunter was trying to communicate with her. Sheba smiled at the hunter. She tried to say hello to him she probably sounded like snorting, with her luck, she smiled her elk smile. The hunter laughed as if he was proud of himself for making a baby noise.

He stepped slowly closer to Sheba and held out his hand. Sheba knew that he was trying not to frighten her, so she slowly stepped closer to him. The man smiled at her again and blew on his stick. Again, it sounded like a mother calling to her child. Sheba didn't know that the hunters could make such sounds. Especially sounds of children playing as well. "Hello friend." he said stepping closer. He looked like he wanted to jump up and down with delight. She recognized the clues because she was showing them herself. He slowly reached up and placed his small hand on Sheba's neck and rubbed her softly. Sheba smiled at the small hunter and nudged him with her nose.

The hunter laughed and patted her neck. "Friend." he said softly. Sheba didn't understand what he was saying, but it sounded friendly to her. The different man slowly caressed Sheba's warm cheek and smiled.

He once more played the child sound and pointed to Sheba. But this time when he played the mother song of sadness, he pointed in the direction that Sheba thought, her family went and where they were to meet. Does he want to help? she thought.

Suddenly Sheba's nose caught a scent riding on the air that made her hair stand on end! "Oh no!" she shouted, "Another hunter is coming!" She quickly jumped to her shaking feet, looked at the small hunter and ran. He watched her run, looking confused on what had just happened.

Sheba had never been so frightened in her life: her father or mother had always been around in times of danger. She could always see, smell, or hear someone she knew, nearby. Now she didn't know if they were even alive.

She continued to run through the trees as fast as she could, backtracking and circling again like her father had taught her. She ran until she could no longer stand. When her legs would not listen. She had stopped in a place with thick grass to lay on. She could hardly catch her breath, she had run so far, so fast. She looked around nervously, she didn't recognize this part of the forest. She had never been here before. Her fear and heart jumped. Her skin swept with cold chills from her nose to her tail. It was darker here and she was lost.

Suddenly she caught a shadow out of the corner of her eye. Now she was really scared. She slowly turned her head in case the shadow hadn't seen her yet. Sheba's big brown eyes got even bigger, she could not believe what she was seeing, she didn't know if it was real. Standing in front of Sheba, was the dark figure of Elkapella. When he moved his form seemed to shimmer with fire and smoke. With no smell.

Elkapella lifted his arm and extended it towards Sheba. "Don't be frightened Sheba," his voice like the breeze blowing through a tunnel of trees. "I am here to help you."

Sheba was astonished that Elkapella knew her name, that he was really there, and he knew her name. She knew she looked nervous. She slowly stood on her shaking legs. She had dreamed of this moment all her life. "H, h, hi." she stammered.

Elkapella moved closer until he was face to face with Sheba. He moved like a leaf drifting in a slow breeze. "What is it you wish Sheba?" he said quietly.

Sheba felt the fear and rage grow deep inside her as she thought back to what happened to her family in the meadow, she thought of the hunters running after them, and she thought of the different man. "I don't know what to do great Elkapella!" she pleaded. "I don't even know where my parents are!" she cried. She could feel her rage growing "Hunters came into the forest and for no reason. shot at my father!"

Elkapella could not give her the council she needed. But he had other ways.

First, he gifted her to ease her heart, a calmness she desperately needed for his next gift.

Elkapella knowing she would not hear most, he explained to her, that the hunter's needed the animals for food, just like the Elk needed the grass. He also told her that if the hunters didn't take some of the animals, the herds would grow too large, and that some would eat it all and in the long winter everything will be eaten too quickly. Many more of her friends would die. Many more than the hunter's now take. He reminded her of the stories she had been taught of how the man and the other creatures had changed when given knowledge.

Sheba looked confused and angry. "If only I could hunt the hunter!" she said angrily.

"Oh, you'll do better than that." Elkapella whispered placing a ghostly hand on Sheba's shaking shoulder. She felt heat from his hand immediately rush through her body. Her hair stood up all over her long, tall body. She was swiftly emerged in a brilliant white light. Sheba held her eyes tightly closed as the heat and light grew. Her body grew hot, she tingled all over. Like she was being stabbed by thousands of tiny thorns.

Chapter 6

A NEW ARRIVAL

 HEN THE HUNTING PARTY returned to the village, Eagle-heart talked to his grandfather about his experience with the Elk. He went to help and watch as his father and the other hunters worked on the animals they had brought back, while his grandfather played his flute by the crops, to help them grow.

Elk-grandson has taught his son how to harvest and skin all the animals. He was learning which parts to use now, what to dry for later and how to use the smallest part. Nothing is wasted. His father taught him how to work the stomach from the animals to make bags to hold water. Eagle-heart, worked by his father nervously, his mind racing, running over and over his unique run in with the elk.

His father was grunting with more frustration than usual; Eagle-heart knew his father was angry that he was one of the hunters, that did not harvest a large animal. He felt like less of a man, he had not done his part for his people nor his son. He felt less of a father.

"Father," Eagle-heart, asked quietly not wanting to upset him more. "I am happy that we use all the parts."

Elk-grandson stopped scrapping the fat from the hide and looked up to his son. "Yes, my son," he said patting Eagle-heart's head. "We do not want to waste anything; we use all that we can." He held up a stringy piece. "Even the sinew to make tough string and more." He smiled. "What do you think your bow string is made of?"

Eagle-heart looked up when he saw his grandfather walk quickly by. He was staring towards the tree line at the edge of the village. Eagle-heart stood up to see where he was looking. "Excuse me father," he said standing up. "Can I go and talk to grandfather?"

Elk-grandson his head filled with his own thoughts and busy working; he was not paying attention. "Um... Yes, whatever you need to do." he waved him off. The Koka and Eagle-heart walked through the village. The Koka pointing out little things, differences, and people.

"No one sees the same things, in the same ways." The Koka explained. "The fish does not see the same world as the groundhog, and he does not see the same world as the eagle. You need to try your best, to always think from the others perceptions and memories."

Eagle-heart shook his head, "I wish my father could forget this year's hunt." "Your father will remember not getting an elk this year for a long time. Your memories are what shape your life, they shape you into who you are. He will be a better man for it" The Koka, put his hand on his young pupil's shoulder. "See that big man sitting over there?" He gestured, "One with lighter skin and thick face hair." Eagle-heart looked over to see the hairy man sitting quietly under a willow tree. He was staring into the river, but his look was miles away.

"Yes Koka, I know of him," he smiled. "that's the Storyteller, Bear-Claw, everyone knows him." he snorted, "It's great to sit at his night fire!" he looked up towards the stars. "He tells amazing stories." He looked back at the man.

"What was his name when he first came here Koka?"

"He couldn't remember." He said sadly. "We called him Bear-Claw because of his large hands and a scar across his neck that looks like that of a bear claw."

He looked sadly at the large man. "Something happened to him that took everything from him, including his memories." His thick eyebrows furled.

"And in return, for those stolen memories, it gave him a gift of Stories to share with us."

Eagle-heart's smile dimmed. "Does he know where he came from?"

"No, my boy." he paused taking in a deep breath, "Sometimes his nightmares remember. They remember things that make him cry it out. Pleading to someone to not give up." he turned to face his young pupil. "Sometimes we should be thankful, for things we cannot remember."

The Koka took in a slow deep breath. "Sometimes life gives us something that we do not expect," he stopped. "Like this," He pointed to the tree forest tree line, where there stood a frightened looking young lady.

"Who is she?" Eagle-heart asked. "She looks scared grandpa."

The Koka nodded and took a puff of his pipe and blew out a skiff of smoke. They both watched it closely as the special smoke swirled into a shape. The rolling smoke pointed toward her. "She is someone very special," he said placing his hand on Eagle-heart's head. "And she has been sent here. She was sent for a very special reason." He smiled.

The woman was looking at the village like she hadn't seen anything like it before. She just stood there, frozen like a frightened deer. "Wait her," the Koka said softly. "I must help her."

She had long straight hair that waved slightly in the breeze. Eagle-heart noticed it was lighter in color than the hair of his people. He had only seen that a few times. She was wearing strange clothes that looked like they were made completely of Elk hide. He watched his grandfather as he carefully approached the woman. He could not help but laugh a little. His grandfather, the great Koka, looked like he was approaching a scared animal in a trap. The Koka stopped a few feet in front of her and began talking. Eagle-heart tried to stretch out his hearing, but it was no use. There was no way he could hear what they were saying.

Before long, the Koka and the woman walked hand in hand back to where Eagle-heart was waiting. "This is Sheba," he introduced her. "She has come a long way to learn our ways." He unusually placed her hand into Eagle-hearts.

"This is my grandson, Eagle-heart." He was smiling ear to ear.

Eagle-heart was astonished; he knew that he had met her before, he was sure of it. Her eyes were the biggest and the most beautiful color of brown he had ever seen. He knew that he knew those brilliant eyes. He could never forget those eyes.

Her eyelashes were amazingly long, and her skin was so fair and soft, he didn't want to let go of her hand. It reminded him of moms holding their children's hands around the village. He had not had that special bond, at least as far as he could remember. And Sheba did not seem to be bothered by holding his hand either.

"Hello Eagle-heart," she smiled in a soft soothing voice. "That is a beautiful name." She knelt to look him straight in the eyes. "It is a name that fits you well." she smiled warmly. "I can see that your heart can love as far as the eagle can see." She reached up and touched his soft cheek. "It is a pleasure to see you again. Friend."

Eagle-heart's legs started to shake, he knew who she was, and where he had meet her before.

Before he had a chance to say anything, his grandfather seen the look in his eyes. "Eagle-heart." he said quietly. "We have a secret to keep don't we." he placed his fist on his grandson's shoulder and winked.

Eagle-heart's mind was racing. He not only could not believe what he was seeing, he wasn't sure it was really happening. He was scared, baffled, and excited all at once. "Yes Grandfather," he gulped,

"Um, Yes, I guess we do." The Koka turned to see many of his people that had seen the new arrival and were walking over. The Koka went to them, leaving Eagle-heart alone with Sheba.

"So how, why...what is going on?" he stammered trying to ask her all his questions at once.

Sheba placed her new hand on Eagle-heart's shoulder. "I'm not sure my young friend," she said quietly. "But Elkapella, must have a reason." she hesitated for a moment, not wanting to sound threatening. "Where is the big hunter you were with today?" she asked. "Who is he?"

"Elkapella?" his excitement grew. Eagle-heart looked towards the men who were attending to the harvested animals. "He is over there," he pointed his dirty little finger at the group of men. "He is helping the other hunters cut meat."

Sheba, quickly turned away from it with horror. Desperately trying not to throw up. She needed to find the hunter to know what happened to her father.

She took in several deep breaths, concentrating, trying to calm her anger, she was sure Elkapella, had more of a reason to send her here. She had to endure it.

The people were gathering around them. "My friends," the Koka raised his voice to be heard. "This is Sheba, and she traveled far to see us." He placed his hand on her shoulder. "She doesn't know how she got here; we must care for until she can find her way." He looked at her knowingly, "Maybe it will help her remember if we teach her our ways. Teach and care for her as one of our own."

Sheba looked at every man's face that she could see, but the curious women gathered quickly around her.

Elk-grandson kept back, watching from afar. Although, like the other men, he was very interested in her. He had never seen such a woman before; he could swear she even had a glow around her. He realized that she had started to stir feelings in him that he hadn't felt since the loss of his wife. Feelings he thought he could never feel again. He shook his head; he should not be thinking this way. Even though he did not harvest any big game, there was still much work to be done. He pulled his eye's reluctantly from Sheba and went back to work. The crowd dissipated as the women led Sheba to where they were working.

They passed people weaving baskets, mending clothes, some doing beadwork and another carving a flute. Sheba was amazed they could do such wonderful things with these hands and these fingers. She looked at her new fingers. So many things she could never do with her hooves.

Her revenge all but forgotten, Sheba sat within the women for hours, learning everything anyone would be willing to teach her.

A woman who had befriended Sheba, took her by the hand. "Come on," she said excitedly, "it is time to gather around the after fire!" she pulled Sheba to her feet. "You have got to see this!" she said dancing a little. "This is a most important ceremony!"

Sheba was dragged to a gathering of people around a giant fire. When she got to a place she could see through the crowd, she found she was standing next to a very shiny and a very large rock. She couldn't help sliding her hand along its smooth surface. It was of a shape she had never seen. Sheba was very frightened being so close to the fire, with so many dancing and bumping into her!

Sheba looked at her, feeling confused. "What is that dancing?" she asked.

Now it was Chanta's turn to look confused. "You mean your people never dance?" she asked, waving her arms in the air, and twisting her shoulders back and forth.

Sheba watched her new friend's movements and was more confused. "Maybe our word for dance is different." she said hoping to get a better answer than flaring arms.

The music and mood changed; a line appeared as the hunters moved strangely around the council fire. They were jumping, swinging their arms, and shouting strange sounds and blowing on their flutes. She watched as the light from the blazing fire, flickered on their painted body's, making them look as if they were moving in slow motion.

The people who were sitting in a circle around the fire, were also shouting strange sounds and when the fire flickered across them, their faces were full of joy and excitement.

The fire let out a roar as it blasted higher into the darkening sky. The smoke split and separated in front of her, and she could see the Koka was sitting on the shimmering, smooth boulder that was now across from her. His legs were folded under making his eyes look solid white. His wrinkled, lip were moving in a silent murmur. Suddenly his eyes dropped. He was looking right at Sheba.

Sheba could feel his eyes burning into her, as if he was seeing right through her. She was frightened by feeling and the look on the Koka's face he lowered his arms toward the smoke, never taking his eyes from Sheba. His fists started circling around and around, he took in a deep breath, and blew out sharply.

The dark smoke twirled into a tunnel of smoke that shot out, straight at the terrified Sheba.

The dense smoke burned Sheba's eyes, she quickly tightened them, and couldn't help but gasp. To her surprise the smoke didn't choke her as she inhaled. The smoke seemed not to head to her lungs but to her heart, mind, and eyes in a warm, embracing numbness. It was not smoke.

Sheba started to feel hot from the tips of her toes to the ends of her hair.

New feelings started to stir deep inside her, and she slowly opened her eyes. It was like she was looking through someone else's eyes, she could see things she couldn't before. Seeing through man eyes was different enough, but this wasn't the same kind of sight.

The smoke from the fire was full of animals, from her cousin the great moose, all the way down to small fish that swam through the smoke water. That's what the people had been looking at. Sheba looked at the hunters, they weren't just jumping crazily around the fire, they were dancing, dancing beautifully to show respect and courage to their forest brothers. Sheba could also hear things she couldn't before. The people weren't just shouting strange sounds they were singing songs, songs of their great thankfulness to the animals who gave their lives, to preserve their own.

Sheba, watched the young boys who went with their fathers on the hunt as they joined in. She saw her young friend Eagle-heart, she could feel his love and gratitude flow from him, into the surrounding energies, as he danced joyfully around the blazing fire. Sheba looked around at the women who were gathered around her, their arms and legs were folded, and their heads were bowed. She could feel what was coming from their hearts and minds as well. They were praying to a higher power. A power that sent them Elkapella.

Suddenly through all the feelings of good, she felt a strong feeling of torment.

Sheba stood and wondered where these mixed emotions were coming from. At the edge of the gathered people, the fire light flickered, and Sheba saw a hunter sitting in the shadows alone. The hunter's legs were folded like the others, but his face was lowered into his hands. She stepped closer and searched through his feelings. His feelings in his heart and mind did not match. His mind was filled with anger, hatefulness, and revenge but his heart filled with loss, loneliness and more love and compassion than Sheba had ever felt before. As Sheba searched his heart, she couldn't help but to be drawn into it. Suddenly the hunter looked up and when their eyes meet, Sheba felt their hearts intertwin as one.

The hunter's eyes went wide with surprise, he quickly jumped to his feet.

"Sheba," he mumbled shyly. "I didn't see you there."

"You know my name?" She blushed.

"Yes," replied the hunter nervously. "You are different from the women in our village."

Sheba smiled warmly. "More than you know." she giggle.

He looked down at his feet and shuffled like a nervous boy, then quickly lifted his head, and tried to look strong and brave. "I, um, would like to know you." he stuttered and had a look of longing in his eyes.

Sheba felt her cheeks get hot as they blushed for the first time. "I am honored to finally meet you, Sheba, I'm Elk-grandson."

Sheba's big brown eyes grew even bigger. "That is the best name I have heard here," she almost shouted. "How did you get such a great name?"

Elk-grandson looked at the people that surrounded the fire. "I don't know," he said with a hint of anger in his voice, "my father has told me many times why, but he leaves something out." He was frustrated. "The important part to my name song is missing." He looked down at his feet again. "When I was young, I liked my name," he said bitterly. "But now it's different."

Sheba felt his heart and mind start to struggle again. She reached out and lifted his strong chin and looked into the depths of his eyes. "Elk-grandson is the most honorable name anyone could have." she said softly. "Trust me." Her smile melting his iced-up feelings.

He smiled and she could feel the love and compassion start to grow, starting to refill his heart again. She saw it in his eyes and when he blushed, she knew that he saw it reflected in her own big eyes.

Sheba and Elk-Grandson spent the next few days hardly ever apart. The smiling Koka hidden from sight, but never too far away. His lessons with Eagle-heart kept most his time, and Elk-grandson, took most of hers. Elk-grandson missed much time with his son. When he had time to see his son, she was learning a new craft or some other woman thing. Strangely in those short days, he never had the chance to introduce Sheba to his son. It seemed like whenever Eagle-heart was around, Sheba was off with the women of the village and when Sheba was by him, Eagle-heart was always in Koka lessons and when he wasn't he was spending time with a new friend.

Every day their hearts grew closer as they talked and shared time together. In those joyful days, Sheba still couldn't figure out why Elk-grandson, struggled so much between his heart and mind. His mind was angry with something that his heart couldn't truly believe.

While walking by the strange great rock, Sheba took Elk-grandson's hand in her own and looked him straight in the eyes. "What is this anger you hold locked in your thoughts?" she asked softly not wanting to say the rest. "Does it have something to do with the loss of your wife?" Sheba cringed inside at her own words, she cringed as she waited for an answer.

Elk-grandson looked over at the engraving of Elkapella, Sheba could feel his anger rise. She expected him to drop her hand, but instead he squeezed it tighter. Sheba looked over at the carving he was staring at. "Does it have something to do with Elkapella?" she asked.

He took hold of her hand. "Do your people believe in Elkapella?" he asked.

Sheba, wanted to wipe away the tear that fell from his eye, but she knew how proud he was. Sheba knew it would make him feel less of a man. "Yes, we believe in him very much," she said. "He is the one who lead me here."

Elk-grandson sat down and gently pulled Sheba down next to him. He tried to speak several times but couldn't seem to get it out. She could feel that he was fighting the turmoil inside himself.

"What is it?" she asked placing her hand on his cheek. "You can tell me anything."

He tried to smile, stood up and paced in front of her. "When I was young, my father taught me the ways of Elkapella," he said bitterly. "And I believe him, I swear I thought I could even see him sometimes." He kicked a rock on the ground and shook his head. "He taught me that the animals of the forest were our brothers." he continued. "I even taught his ways to my own son." He slammed his fist against his chest. "I was to become a Koka!" he cried. "But I was wrong!"

"But it's not wrong," Sheba said standing up desperately, wanting him to believe her words. "The animals live in circle and balance with your people." She wanted to say more but didn't want to anger him further. He felt on the verge of something.

He stopped pacing and looked at her. "I was wrong," he said angrily. "And I'll tell you why." He folded his arms and lowered his head. "I'm sorry for shouting." he said calmly. "A few years ago, when I was hunting with the others, the women were out gathering, including my wife." He shook his head and wiped a tear from his eye. "My wife and son were gathering berries by the river."

"Eagle-heart was very small back then, he was playing while my wife gathered deeper into the thick brush." Elk-grandson paused and took in a slow deep breath. "When we came back the women were frantic, and one was holding my son. They quickly led us to where I learned how wrong I was." He looked up at Sheba and took in another deep breath. "My wife was lying on the ground; she had been mauled by a bear. Over berries."

Chapter 7

FINAL UNDERSTANDING

SHEBA'S HEART SANK, she knew how much Elk-grandson loved his wife and now Sheba loved him too. She couldn't stand to see him this way but at least now, she finally understood. She threw her arms around him and started to cry with him. "I'm sorry," she whispered. I wish that I could fix the hole in your heart."

Elk-grandson hugged her back and stroked her long, soft hair. "You have already started too." he whispered.

Suddenly something that Sheba's mom had told her leaped into her memory. She quickly pulled back but kept her arms around him. "I remember," she said.

He looked very confused. "What do you mean?" he asked wiping a tear from his cheek.

"I remember the bear attack!" she said some memories came flooding in, things that her mom had told her. Elk-grandson looked at her more confused.

Sheba pulled herself out of his arms and started to pace. "I remember my mother telling me about her friend." She said pausing as she tried to think of a way to tell him what she knew and not who she was. "My mother told me of a bear and her small cub that once lived not far from here," She looked sad as she continued. "My mother said they were eating berries and the mother went to see if the river was low enough to catch fish. When the mother returned, she could not find her cub, but she could smell the scent of a hunter. She was very frightened. I can only imagine how frightened she was."

"Frightening to a bear!?" he shook his head looking as if she gone crazy. "How could they know what the bear smelled or how she felt?" he asked bitterly. "They are uncaring beasts."

Sheba hesitated trying not to take offence. "This is just what my mother told me. The mother bear looked frantically for her cub, calling out for him, and getting more freighted. With every frantic pounce, the hunters scent grew stronger. The brushes next to her opened and with her mother's instincts kicked in before she could think, she attacked. When she looked down, and what she saw filled her heart with sorrow. It wasn't a hunter she smelled; it was a female with a basket of food. Her cub had been safe. She didn't know."

Sheba looked over at Elk-grandson, he was shaking his head and pacing again. "How could this be true!" he shouted, "How could your people know this for sure?" He stopped pacing and put his hands on his cringing face. "Did I really lose her because of a mistake?"

Sheba embraced him and he squeezed her tightly with his strong arms. "The story I told you is the truth," Sheba whispered softly. "I am truly sorry." Elk-grandson held her tighter. "I trust you Sheba," he whispered back, "I don't know how, but I believe you." He shook his head, stunned by the absurdness of it. How could she possibly know? He looked into her big brown eyes and melted. "If you say something is true, I will always believe you." He let go of her hand, reached down, picked a flower, and placed it in her hair.

They both turned when they heard shouting. "Sheba. Sheba!" called the small voice. Eagle-heart was running towards them. Sheba let go of Elk-grandson, just as Eagle-heart threw his arms around her. "Where have you been?" he asked. "We were supposed to go for a walk remember!"

"Sorry," Sheba said ruffling his hair. "I forgot."

Elk-grandson looked at them both and smiled. "You know Eagle-heart?" he said excitedly.

"Of course, I do" she smiled. "He is my good friend. Almost every day he has found me between his own lessons. He comes and gets me when I am with the women and drags me off to play." Elk-grandson smiled with pleasure the woman he loves, also cares for his son.

Eagle-heart looked up. "I see you've met my father!" he said excitedly, "He is the hunter that I was with that day." He smiled wider. "My father."

Sheba looked from Eagle-heart to Elk-grandson and back. "Wait," she raised her hand. "Elk-grandson... You, your father was the hunter?!" she gasped

"Sure is!" Eagle-heart shouted proudly.

Now Sheba was filled with turmoil, Eagle-heart's father is the one who took away her parents. Sheba put her hands to her face as she started to cry. She understood these people's ways and how they live in circle and balance with the animals, but how could she be with the man who took away her parents! She pulled the flower from her hair and let it drop to the ground. "I'm sorry!" she cried and ran into the forest.

Elk-grandson watched in disbelief as Sheba disappeared into the trees. He quickly turned to his boy. "Tell me son," he said as calmly as he could, but could not hide his eagerness. "What did you tell her?" his grip tightened. "Why when she found out I was your father, did she get so upset?"

Eagle-heart searched his mind. He knew he couldn't tell his father who or what Sheba truly was, he had promised his grandfather. He was taught to never break a promise and to never lie. "When she first came to our village," he said trying to remember everything he could and not lie to his father. "She knew I had been out hunting that day, and she asked me who I was with." He looked up. "I just told her I was with you, my father."

Elk-grandson thought for a moment and squeezed his son's shoulders. "Is that why she left?" he asked desperately. "Did you tell her that I didn't harvest an animal for our people, does she think me less of a man?" he made a point to not talk about that day, that bad hunt with her. He did not want the first hunt day she meet him on, to be one which he failed.

Eagle-heart shook his head. "No father, she doesn't know that." he said. "She didn't even ask what my father's name was." He searched his mind for anything that might help. "Every time we were together, we would have a good time, I never mentioned the hunt or hunting, and I never thought to tell her your name." He winked, "you are father to me."

Elk-grandson stood up and searched his own memory, he had always talked to Sheba about his son, but he couldn't remember ever saying Eagle-heart's name. Why would she get so upset when he told her that Elk-grandson was his father? She said it was the best name she had ever heard, she seemed to care a great deal for Eagle-heart, he knew that Sheba loved him, so why?...

"Eagle-heart." he said in quiet desperation. "I have got to find her, my son."

"I know father, I can see the love you have for her in your eyes." He gave his father a hug and squeezed him tightly. "It is nice to see it there again."

"I will bring her back," he said ruffling his son's hair. "As soon as I find her." He winked.

Sheba ran deep into the forest half blinded by the tears in her eyes. She ran until she bumped into something, someone.

"Are you OK my dear?" asked a familiar voice.

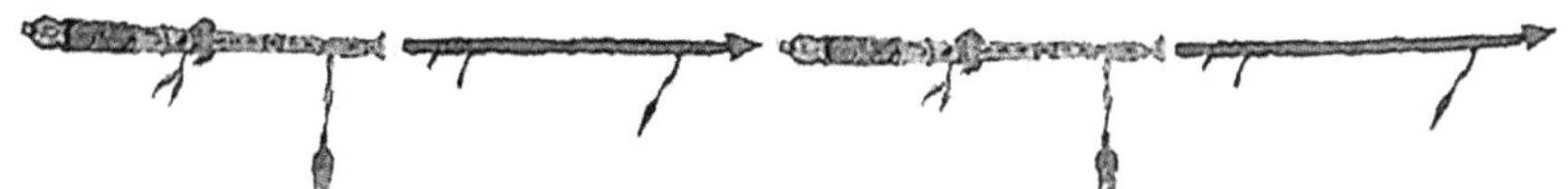

She looked up to the blurred, ghostly figure. It looked solid but seemed too wavier in the breeze. She wiped the tears from her eyes, it was the man Koka. "I'm sorry," she sobbed. "I didn't see you there, I was running, I couldn't, I couldn't...."

"It's OK young one," he comforted her. "I know what you are feeling, and I think I can lighten your burden." He looked into her eyes, "you just need to trust me."

Sheba looked up into the old man's knowing eyes. "What do you mean?" she sniffled.

"Elk-grandson did not harvest an animal on the hunt this year," he said placing his clenched fist on her shaking shoulder. "Your parents are alive and doing quite well."

"What!" She threw her arms around the Koka. Her eyes filled with tears as her heart filled with joy.

"They are waiting for you in the meadow just through the trees." he pointed, "Elkapella, is with them."

"Oh, thank you! Thank you!" She cried hugging him again. As an elk so could never hug like that before, it felt nice. "Thank you so much!" She let go and bolted through the trees.

Sheba ran threw the thicket, her heart beating so rapidly it felt like it was going to burst out of her. She suddenly erupted out of the trees; she saw her parents standing in the clearing with the dark figure of Elkapella.

"Mother, Father!" she cried. She ran to them and threw her arms around their large necks. "Oh, I missed you so much," she sobbed. "I thought I would never see you again!"

"They know everything that has been happening to you," Elkapella said in a wind, deep voice. "They have even been watching you." Elkapella placed his ghostly dark hand on Sheba's shoulder.

She immediately felt the heat rush through her body as it did before. The heat grew and she tingled all over, but she didn't change back into an Elk. "What's wrong," she said in wonder. "Why am I not changing?"

Elkapella seemed to smile. "Your feelings in your heart and mind do not match," Elkapella said softly. "They are filled with torment; your energies do not know where to move." He shimmered like he was smiling. "You want to stick around for a while I think." He laughed.

Sheba looked back in the direction of the man village, then back to Elkapella. "What do I do?" she asked as a tear fell from her cheek. "I don't understand!" she sobbed.

"Go and talk with your parent's, granddaughter," whispered Elkapella, "they will help you." Sheba turned and started to walk with her parents when she realized what Elkapella had just said.

"Granddaughter!" she exclaimed quickly look flashing between the legendary figure and at her father. "It was you! You were there?" she shouted. "You were the young bull elk in the legend?"

Her father nodded; his large antlers broke a branch off a tree. She looked over at the great Elkapella, "And you," she stammered, "are my grandfather?!"

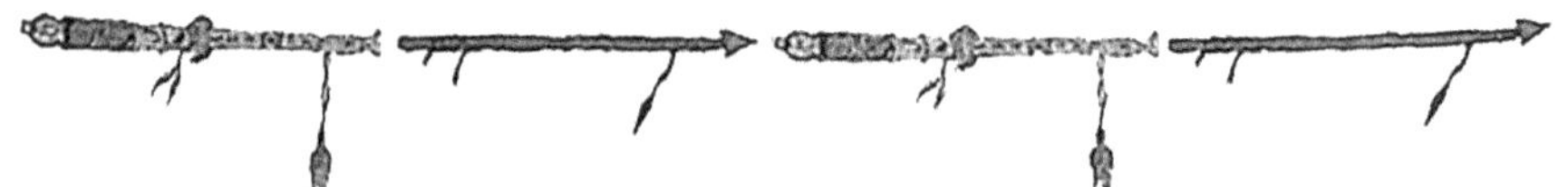

Elk-grandson ran through the forest as fast as he could, stopping only to check the ground for sign of Sheba's passing. The wind began to pick up and started to raise the fallen leaves around him circling in the air. He stopped. He had never seen the wind do this type of whirlwind before. He looked around at the trees, to his surprise none of the branches were swaying.

"Don't be frightened young hunter." came a whisper out of the wind.

Elk-grandson looked furiously around trying to see if his ears were playing tricks on him. The shadows started to gather. They twisted and twirled and grew to the black fiery form of Elkapella.

"Sheba is near and safe," whispered Elkapella. "She is waiting for you Elk-grandson."

Elk-grandson's legs were shaking so bad that he fell to his knees. He couldn't believe what he was seeing. He believed Sheba, when she said the legend was true, but to come face to face with Elkapella was overwhelming. "I'm, I'm so, so sorry," he stammered. "I am so sorry for doubting in you, I have been so, so wrong."

Elkapella placed his dark shadowy hand on Elk-grandson's shoulder, causing him to slightly jump. "Forgiveness is something I shall always give," he said kindly. "Same as who created me."

Elk-grandson felt his heart grow lighter and he knew he had to forgive himself too. "What should I do?" he asked, a tremble in his voice. "I don't know what to say, all I know is I have to see Sheba!"

Elkapella pointed his dark misty arm. "Go to her," he said. "Her heart and mind are in battle, as is yours."

Elk-grandson looked up at Elkapella. "But why," he asked wiping away a tear. "What did I do to upset her so? I must know to not do it again." He pleaded.

Elkapella placed his dark shadowy hand, back on Elk-grandson's shoulder. Suddenly Elk-grandson found himself drawn away in a vision of time and change. He was seeing things as an eagle, a wide view from above. He saw Sheba as an elk with her parents. He saw them run in fear, and he felt and saw when she changed into a woman. He could feel her anger at the hunter, the one she thought took them away from her.

And finally saw himself with Sheba. They were sitting, talking, and laughing by the river, and could feel the love, that she felt for him. Everything was clear.

With a jolt Elk-grandson found himself back on his knees in the forest, Elkapella floating over him. He jumped up and looked to where

Elkapella had pointed. "I finally understand," he said boldly. "And I know what I must do." Elkapella nodded his large head, his antlers to pass through a tree branch.

Elk-grandson started running through the trees again, his heart was pounding, and his mind was racing until he found the small meadow and the large elk standing in it.

He took a deep hopeful breath, "Are you Sheba's parents?" he asked thinking he must be going crazy. He jumped back when they both nodded. The two elk looked behind them and walked apart to reveal Sheba still in human form.

Elk-grandson still connected, felt Sheba's heart leap with joy at seeing her, her mind now clear.

He ran up to her and knelt down. "Sheba," the desperation deep in his voice. "I don't care what you are, or what I am. I just want to be with you." He reached up and took a hold of her hand. "I love you, Sheba."

Sheba's eyes filled with tears as Elk-grandson held up the flower. A tear fell from her big brown eye as she took the flower. She knelt down with him. "I love you too Elk-grandson." she said throwing her arms around him.

After a few blissful moments, she opened her eyes and could see the dark figure of Elkapella dancing just inside the tree line. His large flute, like his head, tossed back and forth, dancing to the most beautiful melody Sheba had ever heard.

Sheba reclosed her eyes and squeezed Elk-grandson tighter. She felt the heat and tingling soar threw her body once again, but this time it was from Elkapella. This time it came from her heart.

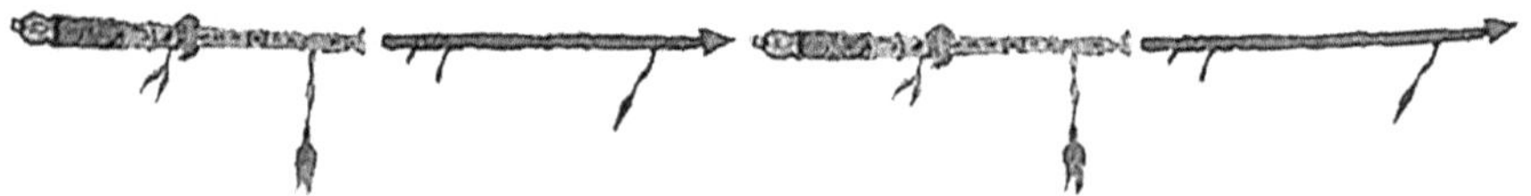

Eagle-heart ran through the forest as fast as his little legs could carry him. He wished he was as swift of runner as his father was. He thought that the majestic elk, how amazing they were, with their great size and massive antlers, they could run through thick timber that he could barely crawl through. Finally, he reached the end of the dark trees and ran out into the small meadow. He stopped dead in his tracks when he saw what was there. The large form of Elkapella was floating right in from of him.

His grandfather standing next to him. His grandfather whispered to Elkapella, Elkapella nodded and together, they waved Eagle-heart closer.

"Grandfather," you know Elkapella he shouted excitedly. "And you talk to him too!" He couldn't help but to jump with joy. He remained reverent.

The Koka smiled at his grandson and chuckled. "Yes Eagle-heart I do," he laughed. "And do you know what else?" he said holding out his normally clenched fist towards his grandson.

"What Koka?" he said excitedly.

"Sometimes he calls me son," he said opening his fist, "sometimes he calls me Pellii."

Eagle-heart stared in amazement. There in his grandfather's open palm, was the undeniable black silhouette, of Elkapella

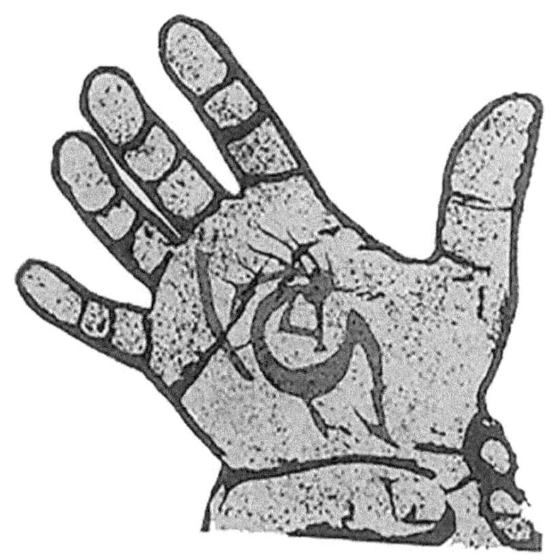

Chapter 8

DREAM?

ORDEN LAID THERE ON THE SOFT mountain ground with places, sounds and scents, rolling through his mind. As he woke up, he opened his eyes to the bright moon light. "When did I fall asleep?" he thought. The last thing he could remember was holding the arrowhead he had just found in front of the center megalith. He took a moment to think and looked around the beautiful mountain. The dream he had dreamt was still on his mind and it was the most vivid and detailed dream he had ever had. He had never had a dream, where he could smell the scents of animals, detailed faces and sounds. He looked down at the arrowhead he still held in his palm. He had squeezed it so hard there was an imprint left in his hand.

As he gazed upwards, he saw something reflecting on the large Center Stone. The Koka Stone, he thought, a smile forming on his face. He slid his hand along the smooth surface until he reached the center. Jorden's smile widened.

He immediately recognized the picture from his dream. From his vision. It was the petroglyph of Elkapella.

He reached into his backpack and pulled a notebook and pencil. He was very excited; he was going to finish the studies he'd started. But now he wanted something new, he also wanted to be, a Storyteller.

About the Author

JB MOUNTEER LOVES HIS FAMILY, writing and telling fun stories. He enjoys the RV life, being in nature & kayaking with his dogs on board. JB loves to meet new characters, listening to their stories, seeing their point of view. He's always up for some rock hunting, karaoke, and traveling. He sees the beauty in everything.